FABULOUS
STORIES FOR
GIRLS

6-in-1 Series
Fabulous Stories for Girls

ISBN: 978-93-5049-426-4

Printed in 2020

© Shree Book Centre

Retold by
Sunita Pant Bansal

Published by

Shree Book Centre

8, Kakad Industrial Estate, S. Keer Marg, off L. J. Road
Matunga (west), Mumbai 400 016, India
Tel.: +91-22-2437 7516 / 2437 4559 / 2438 0907
Email: sales@shreebookcentre.com
Website: www.shreebookcentre.com

Contents

Preface

Fabulous Stories for Girls is a collection of some of the most loved tales in children's literature. Most of these stories have girls as their central characters. This series contains favourites such as the Twelve Huntsmen, the Fair One with Golden Locks, Rapunzel and Cinderella among others. Apart from delighting children, these stories will spark their imagination and help them learn valuable lessons for life.

This book, a carefully picked collection of six stories, is designed to encourage independent reading. Each story is accompanied by colourful, lively illustrations. The simple language makes reading easier for children, and the dialogue blurbs allow the characters to express themselves. The meanings of difficult words at the end of the book will help children improve and build their vocabulary.

The Twelve Huntsmen

Darling, please keep this ring as a token of my love.

Long ago, there lived a prince who was in love with a hunter's daughter. She loved him very much too. The prince gave her a ring as a token of his love.

His father, the king, was very ill. The king told the prince, "Son, I am dying. I want you to be the next king. Promise me that you will marry the girl I choose for you."

The prince promised his dying father without thinking about the hunter's daughter.

Son, promise me that you will marry the girl I choose for you.

When the king passed away, the prince was crowned king. He became very busy with the administration and court affairs of the kingdom.

Soon, his ministers reminded him of the promise. The king sent a proposal to the princess of the neighbouring kingdom, whom his father had chosen.

When the hunter's daughter heard about this,

she could not believe her ears! She was sad and stopped eating and drinking.

Her worried father said, "Don't be so sad! Tell me what you want and I will bring it for you."

The daughter said, "Father, please find eleven girls who look exactly like me in face and body!"

The hunter thought it was a strange request. But he did not say anything. He searched for

Father, I need eleven girls who look exactly like me!

many days and brought home eleven lookalikes.

The hunter's daughter trained her lookalikes in archery and sword fighting.

Once they were trained, the twelve disguised themselves as men and left for the palace. The hunter's daughter asked to meet the king and was led to the court. The king did not recognize her.

The hunter's daughter said, "We are the best huntsmen in the kingdom. Would you like to take us in your service, Your Majesty?"

The king found them handsome and fit. He appointed them as the royal huntsmen.

Now, the king had a talking parrot who was very clever and smart. He said, "Your Majesty! The twelve huntsmen are twelve women in disguise! To prove it, ask your servants to throw some dried peas on the floor of the court tomorrow. If they are men, they will walk steadily. If they are women, they will trip and fall!"

The king could not believe his ears. But he decided to test the huntsmen. Luckily, a loyal servant of the hunter's daughter overheard this conversation and informed her of this. She instructed the eleven girls to walk steadily on the peas.

The next day, the twelve huntsmen walked steadily on the floor of the court. None of them tripped or fell.

The king scolded his parrot. But the parrot said, "Someone must have informed them. Please test them again by placing beautiful, exotic flowers in court. If they are women, they will stop and admire the flowers."

The loyal servant informed the hunter's daughter yet again. She instructed the girls not to stop by the flowers.

The next day, the twelve huntsmen did not go near the beautiful flowers. Again, the king scolded the parrot. As days passed, the twelve huntsmen became the king's favourites.

One day, the court received a letter telling them that the neighbouring princess would arrive soon.

Hearing this, the hunter's daughter fainted. The king rushed to her and pulled off her gloves to rub her hand. He saw the ring and recognized her.

He said, "I am sorry I did not inform you about the promise. You love me truly and went through so much to be close to me. I am sure that the princess will understand that you are the one for me!"

The king sent a letter to the princess of the neighbouring country, telling her about his love for the hunter's daughter. She wrote a letter back wishing them happiness. The king married the hunter's daughter and lived happily ever after!

The Three Little Birds

Once upon a time, there lived three sisters in a cottage near a forest.

One day, a king met the sisters when he was hunting in the forest with two of his ministers. He was charmed by the older sister's beauty and told her, "I want to make you my queen."

The older sister answered, "I will marry you only if your ministers marry my younger sisters." The king agreed. The three sisters got married.

A year later, the king had to go to a neighbouring kingdom. His queen was about to give birth to their child. He told her sisters, "Stay with your older sister till I come back!"

The two younger sisters were jealous of their older sister, because she was the queen. When she gave birth to a baby boy, the younger sisters set afloat the little prince in the river! A bird noticed them doing this.

When the king returned, the younger sisters told him that the queen had given birth to a stillborn baby.

Meanwhile, a fisherman found the baby and raised him as his own.

A year later, the king had to go away again. The queen was about to give birth to their second child. She gave birth to another boy and her sisters set him afloat on the river again. The same bird watched this happen.

Once again, the fisherman rescued the child and raised him as his own.

When the king returned, he was told that the baby boy was dead. The king was very unhappy! The same thing happened for a third time when the king was away, and the bird noticed the younger sisters set the baby girl afloat on the river.

Luckily, the fisherman found this baby as well and raised her along with the two boys.

When the king returned, he was very angry. He ordered that the queen be sent to prison.

Many years passed. The two brothers and their sister grew up to be kind and good looking.

One day, the fisherman told them about how he had found them in the river. Listening to this, the oldest brother went in search of his birth parents.

When they got no news of their brother for a month, the younger brother set out to look for him. When another month passed and neither brother had returned, the sister decided to go in search of them.

It has been two months now since my brothers disappeared!

While looking for her brothers, the sister met an old woman by a stream. She greeted the old woman and asked, "Can I help you with anything?"

The old woman said, "I am a fairy, cursed by a wicked witch. To relieve me, you must cross the stream and find a castle. Then, you must enter the castle and bring me water from the fountain of health. In the castle, there is a golden cage with a bird in it. Bring it back with you."

The girl did exactly as the old woman had told her. On the way back, she found her brothers. They were trapped in the castle, and she rescued them.

Together, they went to the old woman who drank the water and turned into a fairy again.

She thanked the girl and said, "Take this bird with you. It will help you find your parents."

Soon, the king passed by and the bird spoke out loud, saying, "Here is your father, the king. Your mother sits alone in prison for no fault of hers. Her sisters are to be blamed! They were evil. They threw her children away into the river and the fisherman raised them as his own."

When the king heard this, he understood everything. He took his children to the palace and released the queen from prison.

He punished the younger sisters by throwing them into the dungeon.

Blanch and Rosalinda

Once upon a time, there lived two beautiful sisters named Blanch and Rosalinda. Their mother named the elder sister Blanch, because she was fair, and the younger sister Rosalinda, because she had rosy cheeks and lips. The sisters had lost their father when they were very young. Their mother raised them in a small cottage with a fruit garden.

One day, an old woman came to their cottage asking for some water. The mother invited her in and offered her some bread and wine.

Then, the mother said, "Blanch, please pluck some apples from our garden. We will give them to our guest here."

Blanch was a proud and lazy girl. She thought, "Why should I go through all the trouble and treat the old woman warmly?" She gave the apples to the old woman with a frown on her face.

The mother then turned to Rosalinda, "Check if the cherries are ripe."

Rosalinda said, "Mother, the cherries are not ripe yet, but I will bring some eggs for our guest."

Rosalinda ran to the backyard and gathered some freshly laid eggs. She presented them to the old woman with a smile.

The old woman turned into a fairy and said, "Dear ladies, I am touched by your generosity. I will reward the sisters according to their hearts. Blanch, you will be a great queen; and Rosalinda, you will have a big farm." Saying this, the fairy disappeared.

Immediately, their cottage turned into a big mansion with a huge farm outside. It had a big barn with lots of sheep, cows, hens, ducks and pigs. There was also a huge garden with vegetables, fruits and flowers.

Blanch was not jealous of Rosalinda's big farm, for she was daydreaming about becoming a queen. Soon, she heard the sound of horses and ran

to the gate to see who it was. It was the king and his hunting party. The king was so charmed by Blanch's beauty that he asked for her hand in marriage. She agreed to his request, and they got married in a few months.

When Blanch asked Rosalinda to move to the palace with her, Rosalinda said, "This is my house now. I am used to living in the farm."

Blanch was overjoyed that she had become a queen. For the first six months, she enjoyed wearing her grand clothes and attending parties. But, soon, she realized that it was all too troublesome.

She had no friends to confide in, as the ladies of the court gossiped behind her back though they were respectful in front of her. The gossipy

It is so lonely here … I must visit my sister …

ladies wondered what the king had seen in the poor country girl. The king heard what they said and soon, he too began to have doubts about his marriage to Blanch.

Blanch was sad and soon fell sick. She became thin and looked tired all the time.

The royal doctor suggested a change of place, so she went to visit Rosalinda.

As Blanch entered Rosalinda's house, she saw that there was a party going on. Rosalinda rushed to hug her and invited Blanch to join the party.

Rosalinda had married a farmer's son who loved her dearly. Her friends and neighbours loved her for her good heart. Rosalinda grew corn and potatoes on her farm, and her farm

animals gave wool, milk and eggs. She was healthy, happy and content.

Blanch said, "Oh! The fairy gave me a gift which only made me sad. Happiness is found in simple things and not in big palaces!"

The fairy appeared and said, "Blanch, when you became queen, it was not a reward. It was a lesson for your ill will and pride."

Blanch was sorry. She had learnt her lesson well. She did not want to return to the palace now. She stayed with Blanch and her husband, and became healthy and happy.

The Fair One with Golden Locks

Long ago, there lived a princess. She was so beautiful that she was called "Princess Fair One with Golden Locks". She was fairer than the day and her hair shone like bright sunlight. She wore sweet-smelling fresh flowers in her long golden hair. Her gowns were always decorated with precious gems and pearls. Many kings, princes, suitors and admirers wanted to marry her, but she refused them all.

In a faraway kingdom, there lived a rich and handsome prince named Edward. He was also charmed by the princess' beauty and had made up his mind to marry her. He sent a messenger with a marriage proposal and lots of gifts for her. As soon as the messenger left for the princess'

kingdom, Prince Edward started with the wedding preparations. He was confident that the princess would agree to marry him.

When Edward's messenger met the princess, she thanked him for bringing the proposal, but said, "I do not wish to marry now."

The sad messenger took all the gifts that Edward had sent and returned to his kingdom. Prince Edward was disappointed that his proposal was rejected.

One of his trusted courtiers called Avenant, said to him, "Your Majesty, please allow me to convince the princess about your wonderful qualities. Then, she will not have the heart to

refuse you. For that, I just need a horse and a letter from you."

Soon, Avenant set out to meet the princess. On the way, he saw a fish trying to catch a fly. It leaped so high in the air that it fell on the grass.

Avenant felt pity for the fish and put it back into the water. The fish said, "Thank you for saving my life. I will help you when the time comes."

The next day, Avenant saw a large eagle chasing a crow. He felt sad for the poor crow and shot an arrow at the eagle. The crow said, "Thank you for saving my life. I will help you when you most need it."

Sometime later, Avenant noticed an owl crying in pain. It was caught in a hunter's net. Avenant rescued the owl from the net and set it free. The owl thanked him and left with the promise to help in the future.

When Avenant went to meet the princess, she welcomed him warmly, for she had heard great things about him. She said, "Avenant, I am pleased to meet you and request a favour. I lost a ring a month ago in the river. I have vowed that I will not be married until I get my ring back."

So, Avenant went to the river, but he was not sure how to find the ring. Suddenly, the fish

called out, "Avenant, I will bring the ring. You saved my life and it is my turn to help you."

The princess was pleased to have her ring back and said, "Thank you. May I ask you for another favour? There is a giant who lives nearby and is troubling my people. You must fight him!"

Avenant went to fight the giant, not knowing how he would defeat him. But the crow came to his aid, by pecking the giant's eyes, making him blind, helping Avenant defeat him.

Next, the princess asked him to bring the water of youth and health from a cave full of dragons.

Avenant left, with no hope of returning. But

the owl came to his rescue by bringing the water of youth from the cave.

The princess was impressed with Avenant and wished to marry him.

But Avenant said, "I do not want to deceive my prince."

So, she got engaged to Edward. But Edward was jealous of Avenant because the princess always spoke highly of him. So, he sent Avenant to prison. The princess begged him to release Avenant, but he refused.

One day, Edward drank poison instead of the water of youth, and died. The princess released Avenant and later married him.

Rapunzel

Once upon a time, there lived a couple who longed to have a child.

Their neighbour was a wicked and cruel witch. She had a beautiful garden where she grew herbs and vegetables. Since the witch was wicked, no one dared to go near her house.

The childless couple spent their free time looking at the witch's beautiful garden from their balcony.

One day, the wife said to her husband, "The radishes in the witch's garden look so delicious. How I wish I could taste them!"

Her husband said, "Don't even think about it! You know how cruel she is."

But the wife so desperately wanted the radishes that she could think of nothing else. Since she could not get them, she became sad and fell ill.

Her husband asked, "What is bothering you, dear?"

She said, "I want to eat the radishes from the witch's garden. I think of them all the time. If

I don't get them, I will surely die."

The husband was worried about his wife's health. That night, he quietly climbed over the fence and crawled into the garden. He plucked a bunch of radishes and managed to escape. When his wife saw the radishes, she was delighted. She quickly made a salad and ate them all up. She liked them so much that she asked her

husband for more.

So, the poor husband went back to the garden to bring her more radishes. When the husband was plucking the radishes, the witch caught him and asked, "How dare you steal from my garden?"

The husband said, "Please forgive me. My wife longed for your radishes and she would have died if she had not eaten them."

The witch thought for a while and said, "Well then, take as much as you want, but you will have to give me your first born child."

The husband was so scared of her anger, that he agreed to the strange condition and took the radishes back with him.

Soon, the wife gave birth to a baby girl. The witch took the couple's baby away to a forest.

There, she built a tall tower without any doors, just a window on the top. She raised the baby there and named her Rapunzel. Rapunzel grew up to be a beautiful girl with long, golden hair. Whenever the witch left the tower, Rapunzel sang melodious songs. When the witch wanted to enter the tower, she would say, "Rapunzel, Rapunzel, let your hair down."

Rapunzel would let her long hair down for the witch to hold and climb up the tower.

One day, a handsome prince, who was hunting in the forest, heard Rapunzel's melodious singing and said, "I must find the owner of that beautiful voice!"

He came to the tower and saw the witch call out to Rapunzel.

The next day, the prince called out saying, "Rapunzel, Rapunzel, let your hair down." When Rapunzel let her long hair down, the prince used it like a rope and climbed the tower. He fell in love with Rapunzel and asked her to marry him.

Rapunzel also liked him and said, "Bring me some silk every time you come. I will make a rope to climb down the tower."

The prince visited Rapunzel every day and brought some silk with him each time. But the witch soon found out about the prince. She cut Rapunzel's hair and left her in the desert.

When the prince came to the tower, the witch tied Rapunzel's hair to a hook and let it down. The prince came up and was shocked to find the witch. She pushed him off the tower. The prince fell on some thorns. They pierced his eyes and he became blind.

He had wandered for many years till he came to the desert and heard a melodious song. He followed the voice and found Rapunzel. She cried in joy and hugged him. Magically, her tears brought his eyesight back! They lived together happily ever after.

Cinderella

Once upon a time, there lived a rich man who had a daughter. His wife fell very sick and died. She always used to tell her daughter, "Be good and honest always."

Some months later, the rich man married again. His new wife brought her two daughters to live with them. They troubled the rich man's daughter by taking away her best clothes, playing tricks on her and making fun of her.

The poor girl had to cook, clean, wash and light fires. She would get so tired that she slept by the fireplace. She was always covered by cinders and ash. Therefore, she was called Cinderella.

One day, the rich man was going on a business trip and asked his daughters, "What do you want me to bring for you?" His stepdaughters asked for dresses and jewellery, but Cinderella said, "Father, bring me the branch of the first tree that knocks against your hat."

So, the rich man bought beautiful dresses and jewellery for his stepdaughters. On his way back, he broke the first branch that knocked his hat off and brought it for Cinderella.

Cinderella planted the branch on her mother's grave and wept bitterly for her.

As her tears watered the branch, it magically grew into a handsome tree. Every day, Cinderella

kneeled under the tree and prayed. A white bird
on the tree listened to her prayers. The bird was
a fairy in disguise, who protected Cinderella.

One day, when the rich man was away on a
trip, there was an invitation for his daughters from
the king's palace for a grand ball. The stepsisters
were very excited and said, "Cinderella, dress us
in our best clothes and jewellery."

Cinderella did as she was told, hoping that she could go to the palace ball too. But her stepmother refused to take Cinderella, as she did not have a nice dress to wear.

After they left, poor Cinderella sat under the tree and cried, "I wish I had a beautiful dress."

Suddenly, the little bird spoke, "Cinderella! I am your Fairy Godmother. You can have the most beautiful dress and lovely glass slippers for the ball, but you have to come back by midnight."

In a flash, Cinderella was dressed in a splendid dress and glass slippers.

She was excited. She entered the palace and looked around. No one recognized her. The prince was so charmed by her beauty that he immediately asked her for a dance. As they danced, everyone admired Cinderella.

Soon it was midnight. It was time for Cinderella to leave. She ran out of the ballroom without saying goodbye to the prince. She did

not want the him to know who she was.

The prince ran after her, calling, "Wait! I want to know your name."

Cinderella did not answer but just ran out of the palace. While hurrying down the stairs, one of her slippers fell off. But she did not stop to pick it up since she was already late. By the time she reached home, her magical dress had disappeared and she was in her old clothes again.

The prince, who had followed Cinderella, saw the slipper and picked it up. He took it to the king and said, "Father, I will marry the girl whose slipper this is."

So, the next day, the prince and a messenger went from house to house, helping young girls try on the slipper.

Soon, they came to the rich man's house. The stepsisters tried the slipper, but it did not fit them. Just as the prince was leaving, the rich man came back from his trip and said, "Wait! I have another daughter. She has not tried the slipper."

When Cinderella tried the slipper, it fit her perfectly. The stepsisters said, "She can't be the maiden who came to the festival. She is far too dirty!"

But the prince looked closely at her and recognized her. He married Cinderella and they lived happily ever after.

Meanings of Difficult Words

The Twelve Huntsmen

token	:	a gift that is given as a symbol of one's appreciation or love
lookalike	:	someone who looks like another person
archery	:	the art of shooting with bows and arrows
steadily	:	something that is even or regular
exotic	:	something that is beautiful and unusual
scold	:	to speak angrily to someone
trip	:	to hit one's foot on something and stumble and fall
faint	:	to lose consciousness for a short time

The Three Little Birds

witch	:	a woman who practises magic
relieve	:	to become free of pain or suffering
rescue	:	to save someone from a dangerous or unpleasant situation

release	:	to allow a prisoner to be free
dungeon	:	a dark prison that is usually underground

Blanch and Rosalinda

proud	:	think too much of oneself, as if one is greater than others
frown	:	make an angry or unhappy face
backyard	:	the area behind a house
mansion	:	a very large house
barn	:	a large building on a farm where animals or crops are kept
daydream	:	to spend time thinking about something pleasant, especially when one should be doing something more serious
troublesome	:	causing a disturbance or a difficulty
confide	:	to tell someone about something, which they don't tell anyone else

The Fair One with Golden Locks

pity : feel sad for someone

confident : to be sure of something

convince : to make someone believe that something is true

deceive : cheat

impressed : feel admiration or respect for someone

Rapunzel

herbs : plants valued for their medicinal properties

bothering : to give trouble or annoy

delicious : highly pleasant to taste

crawl : to move forward in a kneeling position, using the hands and knees

dare : to be brave enough to do something

melodious : sweet sounding

Cinderella

cinders : burnt pieces of coal or wood

invitation : a written or verbal request that politely asks someone to go somewhere or to do something

charmed : feel pleasure and happiness on seeing someone

maiden : a young unmarried woman